W9-BYZ-014

# TALKIN' ABOUT BESSIE

## *The Story of Aviator Elizabeth Coleman*

BY NIKKI GRIMES ILLUSTRATED BY E. B. LEWIS

ORCHARD BOOKS NEW YORK AN IMPRINT OF SCHOLASTIC INC.

*For* Greenie Neuberg—
Thank you for your spirit
and guidance.

—E.B.L.

*For* Melanie K., who got the ball
rolling, and Rebecca M., who is
becoming her own kind of hero.

—NIKKI



LIBRARY OF CONGRESS CATALOGING-IN-PUBLICATION DATA
Grimes, Nikki.
Talkin' About Bessie: the story of aviator Elizabeth Coleman /
by Nikki Grimes; illustrated by Earl Lewis. p. cm.
Includes bibliographical references.
Summary: A biography of the woman who became the first
licensed Afro-American female pilot.
ISBN 0-439-35243-6
1. Coleman, Bessie, 1896-1926—Anecdotes—juvenile literature.
2. Afro-American women air pilots—United States—Anecdotes—
juvenile literature. [1. Coleman, Bessie, 1896-1926.
2. Air pilots. 3. Afro-Americans—Biography. 4. Women—
Biography.] I. Lewis, Earl, ill. II. Title. TL540.C546G75
2002 629.13'092 [B]—dc21 97-21978

10 9 8 7 6 5 4 3 2 1 02 03 04 05

Printed in Singapore 46
First edition, November 2002

Text is set in 12.5 Joanna MT
Book design by Marijka Kostiw

# Bessie Coleman

was born in Atlanta, Texas, at a time when segregation—with its Jim Crow laws and racist organizations like the Ku Klux Klan—was a way of life in the South, and lynchings of African-American men were commonplace. So-called separate-but-equal schools did little to prepare African-American children to compete in the world of business and academics, because many whites considered African-Americans to be mentally inferior, and descendants of African slaves were only expected to be field hands or factory workers. As a result, there was little talk of technology in the cotton fields of Bessie's world. Certainly, in 1892, when Bessie was born, few African-American people even dreamed of mastering machines that could fly.

Bessie was eleven years old when Orville and Wilbur Wright made the first successful airplane flight near Kitty Hawk, North Carolina, on December 17, 1903. The flight took place on a narrow strip of sand called Kill Devil Hill, a thousand miles from the Texas cabin where Bessie lived. Yet the lives of Bessie and the Wright Brothers are forever linked: all were pioneers in the field of aviation.

Airplanes were widely used in air strikes during World War I, but after the war, civilians had no use for the machines or the pilots who had flown them. Several years would pass before planes were used to transport passengers. Until then, pilots who wished to earn a living flying resorted to performing death-defying stunts, hundreds of feet above the ground, at outdoor circuses. These stunts, or aerobatics, required special skill, steady nerves, split-second timing, and great physical strength, for with each roll, loop, or nosedive the pilot had to fight the natural force of gravity. There was no room for failure because failure often meant death. Not surprisingly, these barnstormers, as they were called, were known for their daring. One of the most daring, and dazzling, of them all was Elizabeth "Bessie" Coleman.

*The form of the following story is fictional,*
*But the story itself is based on fact.*

*Somewhere* on the South Side of Chicago, in a private parlor, twenty souls gather to mourn the death of Bessie Coleman and share their memories of her. Many more had come to the house earlier that evening, but they are long gone. The grandfather clock reads 12:01 A.M., but no one seems to notice that one day has just slipped quietly into another.

*Bessie* eyes the gathering of family, friends, and acquaintances from her place in the photo on the mantel behind them.

"*Hello,* Mama," she whispers. Susan Coleman snaps her head around toward the mantel. She listens for a moment, but there is only silence. Finally, she shakes her head, and turns her attention to her ex-husband, George, who has started to speak.

GEORGE COLEMAN

I remember that bone-chillin' January day in 1892
when Bessie's first cry raised the roof
off that dirt-floor cabin, back in Texas.

Our tenth chile was of a fightin' spirit
and, though four Coleman babies flew to Glory
soon after their arrival, I knew,
of the thirteen born, Bessie would survive.
When she turned two, we moved to
Palmer Road near Mustang Creek
in Waxahachie, Texas,
where Cotton was still King.

The three-room house I built was on
a quarter acre bought with back-
breakin' labor and a careful savin'
few Colored men could manage, thanks
to Jim Crow and the Ku Klux Klan.
A man of African and Choctaw blood,
I was told that hatred was
the only reward to expect in life.

Oklahoma was better suited to prosperity
for such as me. If only my wife had agreed to follow.
'Course, Bessie understood none of that.
She was jus' a chile then, spendin' happy days
waterin' roses, weedin' where corn,
kale, and peanuts grew out back, and
moldin' mud pies after cool spring rains.

Sometimes, I wish I had stayed.

SUSAN COLEMAN

I woke my Bessie before dawn on Sundays
to bathe and dress her for church,
bein' bound and determined that she,
like all my other children,
should first learn the wisdom of the Lawd,
and then, the wisdom of the world.

Bessie got her taste of the second
at school, after she turned six.
I could neitha read nor write,
but fixed it so my children would.
I weekly pinched pennies
to rent books from the library wagon,
which come by the house twice a year.
Still, near as I can remember,
Bessie's first book was the Bible.

Each night, I'd tend the oil lamp,
then sit while Bessie read the Scripture.
Her eyes glowed as they moved across the page.
She'd stumble over the *begats*,
but mostly she'd read in a steady voice,
pausin' between verses to lick her lips
as if the words were honey.
I cried to see the joy Bessie took in readin'.

Somehow, I foreknew the grand use
she would make of it one day

## NILHUS COLEMAN

Bessie had no time for foolishness after Papa left.
There were four of us girls in the house, then, plus Mama.
Lillah and Alberta were long gone, as were John, Walter,
and Isaiah, our three older brothers, which meant,
by the age of nine, Bessie was the oldest child at home.

Overnight, my big sister became a second mother,
who cleaned and swept and cared for us,
while Mama kept another's house crosstown.

Bessie's rag doll rested in a rocker
as its owner braced herself to face
a spring or summer, fall or winter day
of hauling water from the well,
and mopping floors, and making meals atop
the old wood-burning stove that warmed our cabin.

Bessie's days seemed endlessly tiresome to me.
But she just took each one in stride.

# FIELD HAND

Ain't nobody mentioned how crafty Bessie could be.
Not mean-spirited, mind you. Just sly. I saw that side of her,
out in the fields, whenever we were workin' cotton.

Bessie despised pickin' cotton, couldn't even stand the smell,
and she'd show it by laggin' way behind. Once, I even caught her
hitchin' a ride on the back of another picker's sack.

Her mama also caught her at it. 'Course, Mrs. Coleman
let Bessie off scot-free, seein' as how Bessie was the one
who kept the family records and tallied the bales of cotton
the Colemans picked each day, making sure the foreman
paid them their due—and, sometimes, more.

It was an open secret: now and then, as bales was bein' weighed,
Bessie'd "accidently" leave her foot lightly restin' on the scales,
then press down if the foreman chanced to look the other way.

Yessir! You might could say
Bessie bore some watchin'.

# SCHOOL TEACHER

When it came to knowledge, Bessie was a miser,
hoarding facts and figures like gold coins she was
saving up to spend on something special.

I'd watch her sometimes,
poring over her lessons,
lips pursed in concentration.
Often, when the subject turned to math,
she'd glance up at me and, I'd swear,
she'd get a sort of greedy look in her eyes.
But maybe it was just my imagination.

I did not imagine her persistence, though.
Come rain, or shine, if work allowed,
Bessie would attend the hot-in-summer,
cold-in-winter, one-room Colored schoolhouse
where I taught in Waxahachie.
Not even the four-mile walk it took to get there
discouraged her from making her way to class.

Still, bright as she was, I worried that her fine mind
would soon be sacrificed to a life spent picking cotton
or working in the mills, like so many others had before.

But, after each harvest, she'd return to class,
determined as ever to snatch up and pocket
every tidbit of knowledge I could offer.
"Teacher," she'd say, "one day, I'm going
to amount to something."

Bless God! I need not have
fretted in the least.

Folks who met Bessie once she left Waxahachie
considered her allergic to elbow grease and manual labor.
But I recall all the years she took in wash
to help out with the bills, and to fill jelly jars
with precious pennies toward her education.

Laundering was more than just a notion, then.
Talk about some hard work! Listen:
You had to boil clothes in a tub,
scrape and scrub them on a washboard
in a burning bath of soapy lye
that puckered tender skin.

Next came the strain of wringing, and rinsing,
and dipping shirts in starch before
hanging them in the sun to dry.
But your work still wasn't done.

You couldn't call it quits till you'd
pressed each piece with a red-hot iron,
careful not to scorch your fingers.
Your good humor could easily dissolve
in a week's worth of dirty water.

Bessie held her spirits high by saying over
and over again, "I won't be doing this forever."

GEORGIA COLEMAN

# LAUNDRY CUSTOMER

Bessie Coleman? She was a nice-enough girl.
Polite in her way, I suppose. Goodness knows,
I couldn't complain about her work.

My laundry was spotless, perfectly pressed, always delivered
in a timely manner each Saturday, even though my family occupied
a mansion in west Waxahachie, 'bout five miles from the Coloreds.

Bessie had to walk the distance, I believe, but she managed it.
Still, there was somethin' disturbin' about her. I think
it was her eyes. She'd never look *down,* you know?

She'd come to the back door, like they were supposed to in those days.
But when I opened it, there this Colored girl would be standin',
lookin' me straight in the eye, like we were just any two people
meetin' on a street in town. You know, like we were *equals.*

It was odd, I don't mind tellin' you.

OKLAHOMA DRUMMER

I studied at the Colored Agricultural and Normal University,
which was a fancy name for trade school,
and believe me, few people there were rich.
But Elizabeth, as she then preferred to be called,
was among the poorest of our class—though not regarding style.

At eighteen, she studied single-mindedly,
for she did not plan to be a laundress all her life,
or live out her days in Texas as wife to a tenant farmer.

When her money ran out after one semester,
I expected her to show signs of despair. Instead,
she simply wrote a letter home to say she'd be returning.

Soon after, word came that her church had planned
a homecoming party to ease her disappointment.
Her having quit school so early must have been a blow.
Yet, out of nowhere, Bessie got the idea to take the school band
back to Waxahachie with her, to provide the entertainment.

Well, you never saw so much grinning, and hand clapping, and
parading as Bessie did that day at Missionary Baptist Church.

> Only Bessie could turn defeat into a day of celebration—
> and delight in being the star of the show, besides!

ELOIS COLEMAN

My sister wasn't one to take a thing at face value,
especially not thought, or word, or deed to do with race.
*Uncle Tom's Cabin* was among Bessie's favorite books,
and she made it one of ours through her lively reading,
miming a preacher's style so perfectly, we'd be in stitches.

But I recall, after her first recital, she hotly announced,
"I'll never be a Topsy, or an Uncle Tom!"
She had no respect whatever for the slave girl, Topsy,
who seemed incapable of self-improvement,
or for Tom, who had too little race pride
for Bessie's taste. She had no use for either—
not when it came to picking role models, anyhow.

Bessie's habit of probing others' words came,
I suppose, of studying those written by
Booker T. Washington and Paul Lawrence Dunbar.
Sometimes, I wondered how far
their words would take her.

By twenty-three, she'd discovered a newspaper from Chicago
which boasted of a better life up North
and featured stories of powerful women of the Race:
writers, business tycoons, and civil rights workers
like Ida B. Wells, Madame C. J. Walker, Mary Church Terrell—
full-of-hope and headstrong women. Like Bessie.
She'd often wake me at 3:00 A.M., burning to discuss
some new topic or report about our people she'd just read.

I heard the wheels turning in her head long before that
North-bound train rolled through Texas and carried her away.

CURE
for
Coughs
and Colds

## WALTER COLEMAN

My little sister was born for Chicago.
In no time, Bessie seemed to fit right in
with the equally proud and stylishly dressed
ladies and gentlemen of the South Side
who filed through Jessie Binga's bank at lunchtime,
or sauntered by the office of the *Chicago Defender,*
or paraded in and out of countless other
Negro businesses bordering The Stroll.

She loved the salons and haberdasheries,
restaurants and bars, and the nightclubs
like Dreamland, where Louis Armstrong
blew all our blues away.

She'd come North by my invitation,
though she'd always had a mind
to leave the limits of the South.
"You can't make a racehorse of a mule,"
our mother used to say. "If you stay a mule,
you'll never win the race."

Bessie'd planned on winning—
if only she knew *what*.
Each year, she searched for the one trade
or career she thought might best suit her,
never knowing what that vocation was,
or what might lead her to it.

I don't understand how Bessie
kept her focus fixed, but however long it took,
she meant to find a lifelong work of substance,
to prove herself and to make her people proud.

Racehorse or not, Bessie
had a lot in common with a mule.

JOHN COLEMAN

World War One left me with nightmares, and a fondness for drink,
though neitha gave me an excuse for teasin' my sister.
Still, I goaded Bessie 'bout goin' to
the Burnham School of Beauty Culture,
and bein' overeager to avoid
hiring herself out as a domestic.
But she just shrugged. Said she'd had enough
of that kinda work back home.

She got a job buffin' men's nails at
a high-class barbershop on The Stroll,
where I'd drop in to swap war stories
and talk politics with her customers.
I'd point out that she was still a "common laborer,"
after a lifetime of tellin' anyone who'd listen
that she'd amount to somethin' "big" someday.

She'd worked in the shop five years
when I wandered in one afternoon,
blabbin' 'bout airplanes and French women
who had *real* careers as pilots.
Then I turned to Bessie and joked,
"You Negro women ain't never goin' to fly.
Not like those women I saw in France."

The barbershop rocked with laughter.
Then I heard this *snap* that was so familiar:
It was that steel-trap mind of Bessie's.
"That's it," she said. "You just called it for me!"
She gave up her manicurin' job that very day.

That's when I knew: by whatever miracle
was required, Bessie would learn to fly.

ROBERT ABBOTT

Bessie's copper color gave the truth of her away.
For, at the core, she—though slight in appearance—
was tough as any metal, and always ready and willing
to test her strength.
That much was clear the day she strode into my office
to talk about her future and the future of our people.

She was twenty-seven then, and planned to be
the first Colored woman in the world to fly.
The problem was, no flight school
in our color-minded nation
would accept a woman, or a Negro.

She asked for my help, since I, too, had once
been driven by a dream to lift the Race.
I'd founded my newspaper on nothing less.
"Go to Paris," I advised. "French fliers are the best,
and they'll teach anyone. In French, of course."
Much to her credit, Bessie didn't even blink.

I told her of a language school on Michigan Avenue,
and the next I knew, Bessie had enrolled.
For one year, she studied French
and worked in a chili parlor to save toward
the aviation school I found for her in France.

I helped her buy passage on the *SS Imperator*,
and said the *Defender* would promote her cause
*and* record her success—once she returned
with pilot's license in hand.
It was 1920, and Bessie was news,
you understand. As a publisher,
I considered her a wise investment.

When Bessie boarded the steamer that icy November,
she became a front-page story in the making.

*Ja, ja,* she knew a little French, but my English was better.
We would speak together often, for Bessie was lonely.
In a graduating class of sixty-two, she was the only woman,
and the only black, as well, at the Caudron School of Aviation.

Ground school was where our training started, and
Bessie always raced to find a seat up front. She wanted
to be close enough, she said, to catch each new word, and
there were many, like *cowling, struts, joystick, rudder bar*—
all parts of the biplanes we would later learn to fly.

Our heads were filled with principles of flight,
and we were drilled on cloud formations, wind, weather,
and what effect each one might have on takeoffs and landings.
I'd grow dizzy watching Bessie furiously scribble notes.

Sometimes, she would smile and gaze out the window
at the wondrous, man-made birds of wood and wire
silently waiting to lift her up, and up, into the endless
blue over Paris, and she would sigh.

I shared her longing, but not her love for the complex equations
we had to learn: calculating plane weight, plus distance,
and figuring out how much fuel we would need for each flight,
and what the takeoff speed should be—depending on what
the pilot weighs, of course! Juggling such a lot of facts
and figures gave me headaches, but Bessie hummed sweetly,
and puzzled out each problem without complaint.

I asked her, once, to please explain how it was possible
for her to find such difficult work enjoyable.
"As a child," she said, "I was always good at math.
But now, I'm glad to discover that there was, all along,
a higher purpose for my skill than counting bales of cotton."

"What is a bale?" I asked.
Bessie threw her head back and laughed.

CLASSMATE

FLIGHT INSTRUCTOR

*Mais oui*, she was a beauty. A twenty-seven foot-angel
with a forty-foot wingspan—the Nieuport 82,
an old and trusted friend I introduced to students.
But I warned Bessie, as I cautioned everyone,
if she continued her course, the Nieuport could be
the last old friend on whom she ever laid her eyes.

One day, Bessie learned precisely what I meant.
The Nieuport climbed to two thousand feet, then
leveled off, purring perfectly—until the engine quit.
The roar died suddenly away, and soon the plane
was falling, falling, as the wind screamed past.
One hundred, two hundred, three hundred feet it fell,
then snapped into a roll.

Wedges of earth and sky flashed by too fast
for memory as the plane hurtled, then slammed
to the ground with student and teacher on board.
Bessie gasped, watching from the sidelines,
knowing how easily she could be the one in flames.

I was surprised the next day when she came for her
lesson, how she boarded the plane without hesitation.
I signaled directions above the wind and engine roar.
She moved the rudder bar and joystick as I told her,
practicing until her rhythm was steady and sure.

"The crash was a terrible shock to my nerves,"
she later said. "But I never lost them."

NEWS REPORTER #1

It was a crisp autumn day when this reporter
and others gathered at the New York docks
to meet the *SS Manchuria* from France,
there to greet the world's first Colored
aviatrix who was on board.

The lovely lady had traded in blouse and
skirt for a French-cut pilot's uniform, and
had ordered a Nieuport scout plane to be
built for her in Paris, or so she said.

Miss Coleman, I understand, gave
exhibition flights while in Europe,
though I have no proof of such. "They
applauded me wildly in Berlin for my
daredevil skills," she said. "In Munich, too."

A reporter I knew from the *Chicago Herald*
offered to report her story, provided she
would agree to pass for white. However,
her only response to his offer was laughter.

In this reporter's humble opinion,
the *Herald* was the loser, for Bessie
was a spellbinder. She spoke with eyes
and hands and sweeping gestures.
She drew pictures in the air,
and made the listener believe
he was there right inside her story.

Bessie Coleman, aviatrix, could easily
have been a great actress of the stage.

## WILLIE COLEMAN

My sister-in-law shoulda been a writer
since she was always tellin' tales.
Enhancin' the truth was her specialty.
Drummin' up publicity, she called it.

Hear her tell it, she was bosom buddies
with the Red Baron, had flown a German sea
plane, and was near 'bout born with wings.
Told the *New York Times* she went to France
with the Red Cross during the war, and that
she had one of them brigade officers teach
her how to fly. Now, you tell me if
that ain't stretchin' the truth!

Bessie was only five foot three inches,
but she made herself out to be bigger than life.
Who she think she was impressin'?
The kids, maybe. I seen 'em flock to her.
They'd sit round her for hours, listenin'
to her stories. She spoiled 'em, too.
Bought 'em toys, gave 'em spendin' money,
from what little she had. She cooked up
fancy meals for her nephews and nieces.
Made 'em think she was somethin' special.

Quiet as it's kept, I guess she was.
But them dressed-up tales she told!
They hurt more than helped, if you ask me.
Made it harder for folks to believe the plain truth
of what she really did do—which was plenty.

Her causin' folks to think otherwise
was nothin' but a shame.

NEWS REPORTER #2

In 1922, I knew I was in the presence of royalty
when Bessie appeared on that Long Island airfield.
"Queen Bess" had no throne, of course, unless it was
the cockpit of a plane. But we of the press were there
to share in whatever glory came her way.

She received less fanfare and opportunity to profit
from her skill than she deserved. While Amelia Earhart
found sponsors easily enough, Bessie had a tough time
finding companies to fund her exhibitions or hire her
to advertise their wares. Even pilots have to earn a living.

Bessie was not entirely alone in her pursuit.
We of the *Defender* helped to spread her name.
And, though it took a year, we arranged her first
public flight in America. And what a sight she was!
The "gritty and progressive" woman who once worked cotton,
striding regally in uniform and goggles, waving to
us, her royal subjects, who showered her with applause.

Our queen flew a borrowed plane that afternoon,
a humbling necessity, for the company made her
fly once around the field with another pilot
to test her skill before allowing her to fly alone.
I groan at the memory of that insult, even now.
But Bessie accepted it in silence, with grace.

A mere three thousand were in attendance for that performance,
proof that too few of us understood the wonder
of the moment, or the woman. But I still read and wrote
reports of lynchings and was forced to ride
in Coloreds-only railroad cars. I knew how far Bessie
had brought us all. None that mild September day
applauded more loudly, or proudly, than I.

All Hail, Queen Bess!

ROBERT PAUL SACHS

Sachs is the name, Coast Tires is the game.
We paid Bessie a fee to mention our company
during her interviews, making full use of her as a celebrity.
I knew her personally, was honored to be
one of the students she taught to fly,
but I'm especially proud to say that our firm
helped Bessie purchase her first plane.

For my money, I prefer to deal with a person
who knows her own mind, and that was Bessie.
By the time we met, she knew precisely what
she wanted: to start a school of aviation in America
where Negroes could learn to fly.
That was her greatest dream, and owning a plane
would help move her one step closer to it.

She bought herself an old army surplus plane
and arranged an exhibition at Palomar Park in Los Angeles.
Ten thousand gathered for the event, but it was not to be.
On the way from Santa Monica to the airfield,
Bessie's engine stalled three hundred feet above the ground.
The sound of the crash was heard for miles.

For three months, she lay in a hospital,
impatient for her broken bones to knit though
unwilling to quit the sky, for she believed
our people could—and should—succeed
in the world of aviation, and she wouldn't give up
until she had convinced us of it.

I visited her during the difficult recovery. She just
smiled through the bruises and bloody bandages,
painfully propped herself up in bed, and,
whispering, ordered me to spread the word:

> "Tell them all, as soon as I
> can walk, I'm going to fly!"

## YOUNG FAN

You shoulda seen her! She made her plane do spirals and fancy flips,
and made the plane quit, mid-air, and let it zoom down, like when
she crashed in California, and just when we thought she was surely
done for, she pulled the plane up again, and tore off for the sun!

Just think: we Colored folks almost didn't get to see her, 'cause the
air circus was usually Whites-only. But Bessie told the producers
if we couldn't come to the show, she wouldn't either! Her shows
were worth so much money, they finally let her have her way.

Folks here in Waxahachie lined up for a chance to fly with Bessie
after the show, like folks had done in Houston, Memphis, Richmond,
and every other city she'd flown in the last four years. I'd have
flown with Bessie, too, but Ma said girls and planes don't go together.

Bessie was thirty-four, which is sorta old, but she was beautiful.
One time, a film company in Florida was plannin' on making a movie
about her, which was no surprise. Ask me, she was a star already.

Bessie gave a bunch of lectures at local churches and theaters to
raise money so she could start a flying school. I went to hear her
talk at one of them, and sat in the front row and watched the films
she showed of her flying over the kaiser's palace in Germany.

Her eyes sparkled when she talked of aviation, and she said that we
should all think about learning how to fly, especially us girls.
"I am anxious to teach you," she said, and I swear,
she was looking dead at me when she said it.

I haven't made up my mind about being a pilot,
but Bessie made me believe I could be anything.

Lord spoke kindly of the eagle and dove, but he also loved
the raven: a strong, mysterious black bird of high intelligence
is she; a creature slighted by many, but cared for by God—
that was Bessie. She stayed with my wife and I at our
Orlando parsonage, and there Bessie renewed her faith.

For two months, she called my wife and me Mother and Daddy,
her own beloved mother being miles away in Chicago, and her
father living in parts unknown. Viola and I were proud
to be family to Bessie, however brief the time.

I'm pleased that she soaked in God's Word while living with us.
Many's the hour I found her reading the Psalms, usually by lamplight.
She saved the mornings for weeding the vegetable garden out back.
Both pastimes, she said, reminded her of happy days in Waxahachie.

We loved her as our own, and were warmed to see her often
surrounded by children who admired her beauty and her bravery.
I prayed constantly for Bessie's safety and was much relieved
when she agreed to end her barnstorming days and promised
to rely more on her lectures as a means of raising funds
for the school she was bent on building. Her mind was set,
she said, on turning "Uncle Tom's Cabin into a hangar,"
where she could, at long last, teach our people how to fly.

On the porch one night, Viola suggested Bessie might consider
opening a beauty shop for extra money. Bessie liked the idea.
She was almost ready to settle down anyway, she said.
Trying out the quiet life might be nice. Someday soon.
I might've believed it—Lord knows I wanted to—but then,
before we went in, I caught Bessie out the corner of my eye:

> She looked up at the sky for
> one last glimpse of blue heaven.

REVEREND HEZAKIAH KETH HILL

# BESSIE COLEMAN

I'll never forget that first time in France.
My knees wobbled when I climbed into the cockpit.
The mechanic cranked the propeller for me, and soon
a fine spray of engine oil misted my goggles,
baptizing me for take off.
I taxied down the runway, praying.

But flying at Checkerboard Field in Chicago was the best.
My family and friends were there in the stands,
cheering me on as I sliced through the air.
Oh Mama! I wish you could've been in the plane
to feel that magnificent machine shudder
with the sheer joy of leaving the ground.

I climbed over a thousand feet that day,
did a snap roll that sent the blood rushing
to my head so fast I thought my eyes would explode.
My seat belt felt like a magnet, pulling on my spine.
I can still feel my hand gripping the joystick,
how my muscles ached from struggling
to hold the plane center. But I didn't mind.

To rest, even for a moment,
weightless and silent, on a cushion of cloud,
near enough the sun to scoop up a handful of yellow
was a privilege more than worth the price of pain.

In the end, I count myself twice blessed:
first, to have experienced the joy of flight;
and, second, to have shared it with others of my race.
I'll say this and no more:

> You have never lived
> until you have flown!

# Elizabeth "Bessie" Coleman 1892-1926

On April 30, 1926, rehearsing for a show in Florida, "Brave Bessie" sat in the back of her plane while co-pilot William D. Wills took the controls. Her seat belt was unfastened so that she could lean over the side to choose a landing spot for a parachute jump the next day. Suddenly, the plane went into a nosedive and then a tailspin, tossing Bessie to her death. The plane crashed and Wills also died. The cause of the crash remains a mystery.

Bessie was thirty-four years old. Although she never realized her dream of opening a school of aviation for African Americans, her accomplishments were considerable. She overcame obstacles of poverty, as well as racial and sexual discrimination, to become the world's first licensed female pilot of African descent.

Bessie learned a foreign language and traveled to Europe not once but twice in order to study aviation and develop the special skills needed to perform aerobatics. She logged thousands of miles across the country as a lecturer to encourage others of her race to enter the field of aviation. She paved the way for other African-American pilots, including Arthur W. Freeman, her nephew, and was a forerunner to African-American astronauts such as Dr. Mae Jemison.

Among the tributes to Bessie Coleman are the establishment of aviator groups such as the Bessie Coleman Aviators Club of Indiana, the commemoration of May 2 as "Bessie Coleman Day" in Chicago, an access road to Chicago's O'Hare Airport renamed Bessie Coleman Drive, and a commemorative stamp issued in 1995 by the U.S. Postal Service as part of its Black Heritage Series.

Bessie Coleman's sturdy faith and determination to reach her goals challenges each of us to push beyond our limitations to pursue our own dreams.

---

## Acknowledgments

The characters in this oral history portray actual friends, relatives, and associates of Bessie Coleman. However, the voices, styles of speech, and characterizations are all imaginary devices used to bring Bessie's true story to life. In addition, several composite characters have been created in order to maintain the chronology of events. Special thanks to pilots Debra Clary and Shirley Russell for their valuable insights, suggestions, and general assistance in guiding me to background materials for this project.

## Source Material about Bessie Coleman

FISCHER, AUDREY. "Bessie Coleman: Flying in the Face of All Odds," *Woman Pilot* (MARCH/APRIL 1995): PAGES 8-11.

HARDESTY, VON, AND DOMINICK PISANO. *Black Wings: The African American in Aviation*. Washington, D.C., National Air and Space Museum, Smithsonian Institution, 1983.

HINE, DARLENE CLARK, ed. *Black Women in America*. New York: Carlson Publishing, 1993: PAGES 262-263.

IGUS, TOYOMI, ed. *Book of Black Heroes*. Vol. 2, *Great Women in the Struggle*. East Orange, NJ: Just Us Books, 1991.

RICH, DORIS L. *Queen Bess, Daredevil Aviator*. Washington, D.C.: Smithsonian Institution Press, 1993.

———. "My Quest for Queen Bess," *Air & Space Magazine* (AUGUST/SEPTEMBER 1994): PAGES 54-58.

SMITH, JESSIE CARNEY, ed. *Notable Black American Women*. Detroit: Gale Research, 1992: PAGES 202-203.

WATERS, ENOCH P. *American Diary: A Personal History of the Black Press*. Chicago: Path Press, 1987.

## Source Material about Aviation

BACH, RICHARD. *A Gift of Wings*. New York: Dell, 1975.

BRIDGES, KENNETH D. *Bridges Aviation Studies*. Seattle, WA: Bridges Aviation Studies Publ., 1973.

COOPER, ANN. "Jody Fulks Sjogren: Metamorphosis and an Aviation Artist," *Woman Pilot* (APRIL/MAY 1994): PAGES 16-18.

SAINT-EXUPÉRY, ANTOINE DE. *Wind, Sand and Stars*. New York: HBJ Modern Classic Series, 1992.